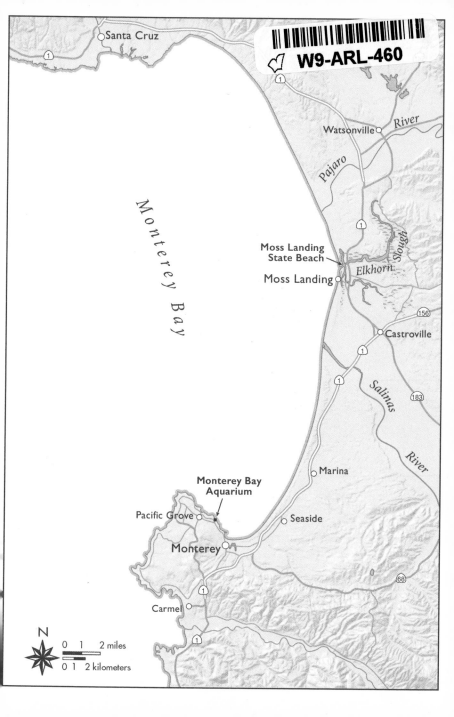

W9-ARL-460

Santa Cruz

1

Watsonville

Pajaro

River

1

Moss Landing
State Beach

Moss Landing

Elkhorn

Slough

Monterey Bay

156

Castroville

1

1

Salinas

183

River

Marina

Monterey Bay
Aquarium

Pacific Grove

Seaside

Monterey

68

1

Carmel

1

N

0 1   2 miles

0 1 2 kilometers

Odder

KATHERINE APPLEGATE

With illustrations by Charles Santoso

Feiwel and Friends
New York

A FEIWEL AND FRIENDS BOOK
An imprint of Macmillan Publishing Group, LLC
120 Broadway, New York, NY 10271
mackids.com

Text copyright © 2022 by Katherine Applegate.
Illustrations copyright © 2022 by Charles Santoso.
Photos on pp. 268 and 270: Suzi Eszterhas/Minden Pictures.
All rights reserved.

Our books may be purchased in bulk for promotional, educational, or
business use. Please contact your local bookseller or the Macmillan
Corporate and Premium Sales Department at (800) 221-7945 ext. 5442
or by email at MacmillanSpecialMarkets@macmillan.com.

Library of Congress Cataloging-in-Publication Data is available.

First edition, 2022
Book design by Michelle Gengaro-Kokmen
Map by Ben Pease, peasepress.com
Printed in the United States of America by LSC Communications,
Harrisonburg, Virginia
Feiwel and Friends logo designed by Filomena Tuosto

ISBN 978-1-250-14742-4 (hardcover)
ISBN 978-1-250-88761-0 (B&N edition)
1 3 5 7 9 10 8 6 4 2

For Liz Szabla,
with oceans of thanks

It is a happy talent
to know how to play.

—*Ralph Waldo Emerson*

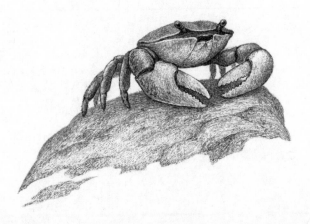

Contents

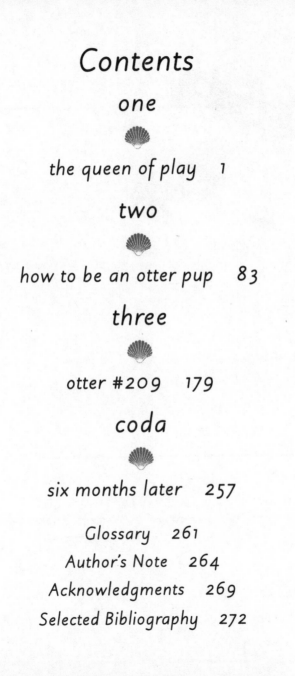

One

the queen of play

Monterey Bay, California
and environs

not (exactly) guilty

In their defense,
sharks
do not (as a rule) eat
otters.

True, sharks sometimes
taste them
by mistake, leaving
frowning bites
or the jagged clue
of a tooth or two.

But then,
in fairness,
nobody's perfect.

too late

Say an empty-bellied
great white shark
is enticed by
a long, sleek swimmer,
a sea lion, perhaps.
(Big fans of
blubber, sharks.)

Curious, the shark
moves in for a nibble,
only to discover he's
sampling a surfer *(oops)*,
or, more likely,
a member of that most
charming branch
of the weasel family,
the southern sea otter.

You've been there,
haven't you,
in the cafeteria line
or the breakfast buffet,

taking a chance on
some new food?
Grab, gulp, grimace:
You spit the offending
item into a napkin,
no harm, no foul.

Same goes for the shark,
who quickly
reconsiders and
retreats.

Of course, by then it's often
too late for the surfer.

And almost always
too late for the otter.

hunger

One such shark
is prowling the waters
this very morning.
It's daybreak,
cloudless and shell pink,
and for a moment the bay
seems to blush.
There it is:
his dorsal fin,
cutting through the
calm waves.

The shark is an adolescent—
a marine tween—
streamlined and strong,
but small for his age,
and far from his usual
haunts today.

His last meal,
a ray and two puny turtles,

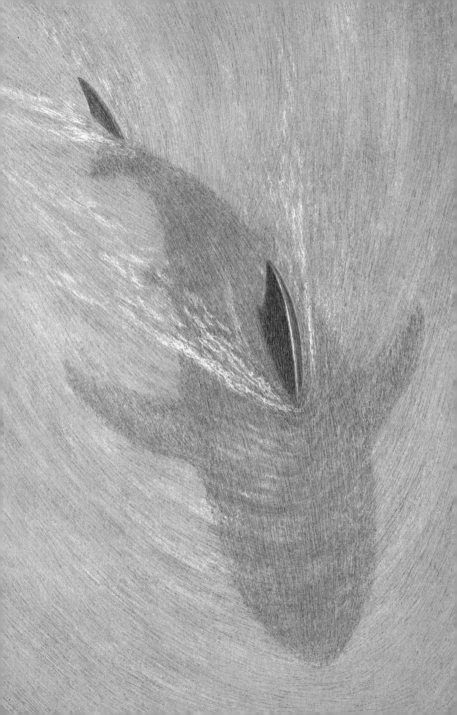

was three days ago—
pathetic, by any measure.

No need to worry.
Hunger has a way
of focusing the mind.

If there is food
to be found, rest assured:
He will find it.

Otter #156

Not far from the shark,
Otter #156 floats on her back,
forepaws and flippers
held aloft,
soaking up sun
like tiny solar panels.

Tucked in a pocket of skin
under her arm
is a favorite rock,
just right for opening
mussels and clams.

She has seen more
than a few sharks in
her three years,
has even seen them
kill.

But right now her only concern
is what to eat for breakfast.

numbers and names

Friends call #156
"Odder,"
but humans prefer
their numbers.

They count cards and sheep,
errors and at-bats,
minutes and blessings.

Here in the bay,
they count
otters, too.

Squiggles and Splash

There's a reason
for those numbers.
Endearing names
enchant the public,
luring humans too close.

Numbers are aloof,
but names are sticky,
fusing rescuer to rescued,
scientist to subject,
human to otter.
(And it's not hard
to fall in love with
an otter pup.)

It's a shame, really.
Think of the possibilities:
Squiggles and Splash
and Potter and Noodle!
Otto and Oswald
and Ozzie and Obi!

Still, it's better this way.
These otters need
all the help
they can get.

questions

Her mother called her "Odder"
from the moment
she was born.

Something about the way
the little pup never settled,
something about the way
her eyes were always
full of questions.

to eat or not to eat

A few feet away
from Odder,
her favorite companion,
Kairi, drifts on her back,
aimless as a log.

Kairi, two years older
than Odder, has
shiny ebony fur.
Odder, smaller
and more agile,
has a deep brown coat
and caramel-colored head.

Play,
Odder wants to know,
or eat?

First we eat,
then we play,
answers Kairi,

who is always practical,
a cautious sort.

It's annoying,
but when you're
a free spirit like Odder,
teaming with a wise
and solid anchor
is never a bad idea.

First we play,
then we eat,
says Odder.

She gives her friend
a soft nose-nudge
and dives through quiet water
thick with eelgrass.

communication

When you cannot text or email,
whisper a secret or
shout a protest,
when words are not your way,
how do you
share what you know?

Otters
whistle and whine,
snarl and hiss,
blow and snort.

And don't forget
sight and scent,
and most of all touch—
nudges and licks,
head butts and gentle bites.

Every species has its tricks.

underwater

Underwater
there's no need for noise,
for grunts or squeals or chirps.

Not when you can twist
and pretzel and weave.

Not when you've turned
frolic into art.

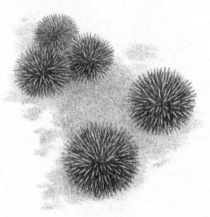

ballet

The chase begins,
through the marshy shallows
of Elkhorn Slough,
toward the icy,
deep waters of the bay—
in, out, up, down,
pirouettes and lifts and dips,
a bubbly ballet.

Far enough,
Kairi says,
when they pause at last.

Their small, smooth heads
could be slick rocks
in a riverbed.

Odder backflips,
disappears,
pops up
a few feet away.

Silly minnow,
she teases,
just a little bit farther,

and the ballet
moves on to Act Two.

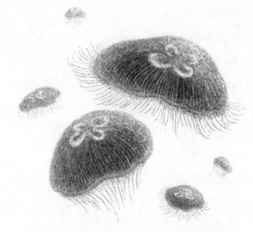

the slough

A slough is heaven
for an otter—
placid and swampy,
with easy pickings.
Just a few feet down
and voilà: your meal.

Of course there are more
humans around—
sightseeing boats,
kayaks and canoes,
everyone anxious to glimpse
the otters and sea lions,
the regal great blue herons
and double-crested cormorants,
the comical pelicans.

the bay

Beyond the slough
lies Monterey Bay,
a whole different animal,
a watery whale,
huge and intimidating,
but breathtaking
beneath the surface:
Kelp forests weave
green blankets
while sun shafts cut
like blades.

Some say the food
is better there—
succulent crabs if you're willing
to work for them—
but the dangers give many
second thoughts.

Not Odder, though.
She loves a good crab.

daily schedule

An otter's life goes like this:
eat
    groom
        sleep
eat
    groom
        sleep
eat
    groom
        sleep

but always there is time for a bit of

deep diving
                      wave chasing
        tail spinning
smooth gliding
                      bubble blowing
           FUN.

the queen of play

Nobody plays like
Odder plays.
Nobody has
her moves.

She loves to roughhouse,
can be pushy and eager,
too unruly for some,
but watching her
work the water
is a joy.

She doesn't just swim to the bottom,
                   she dive-bombs.
She doesn't just somersault,
                   she triple-doughnuts.
She doesn't just ride the waves,
                   she makes them.

diet

The shark, meanwhile,
is closer to the mouth of the slough,
still hunting,
a soundless ocean ghost.

He can eat hugely—gorge,
then go for days unfed.
But a sea otter is always eating.
(Luckily, her belly doubles
as a dinner table.)

Without the swaddling blubber
of a seal or whale,
she must consume
a quarter of her weight
each day—

abalones and sea urchins,
octopuses and sea stars,
mussels and crabs and clams,

like a carb-loading marathoner,
like a hummingbird sipping nectar
dawn to dusk.

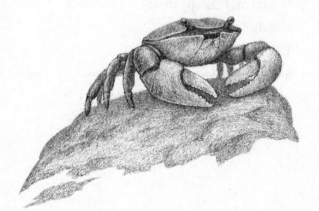

Jaws

No one pities sharks.
There are no great white Bambis,
and that's to be expected,
given that grim smile,
those thousands of
triangular teeth,
row upon
row upon
row.

There are other perks, though:
the way the ocean seems
to part at their approach,
and don't forget the
Hollywood factor—
a movie like *Jaws*
could never be made
about otters.

cute

Still, it's hard,
if you're an ocean resident,
not to resent otters,
their easy popularity,
the way they
woo the crowds.

They are, it's been said,
the champions of cute:
those eyes like a doe's,
the expressive whiskers,
the gold medal
aquatic gymnastics.

And being photogenic
does help with memes, with
keeping the fans
engaged.

Only the foolish
want selfies
with a shark.

kayaker

Odder twists and sees
what she has already
heard and scented:
a human slicing through
the small waves,
half his body tucked
in a hard shell shaped
like a giant sardine.
His awkward churning
—a paddle for paws—
is painful to watch.

She loves kayakers,
admires their hopeless desire
to be what they cannot:
creatures of the water.
Her.

She has visited several,
curious about their
sweating foreheads
and water bottles,

the binoculars they use
for eyes.

The kayaker slows,
and Odder slips underwater,
coming up close enough
to see his white teeth
and smell his exertion.

wary

Odder!
It's Kairi, calling
urgently,
always the killjoy,
ever wary.

Odder!
she calls again.
Keep your distance!

The kayaker makes sounds—
kind ones, Odder decides.
(As it happens,
she has heard her share
of angry humans.)

Still, she does as Kairi
has commanded,
and with a stroke of her tail,
she vanishes from view.

scolding

Sorry,
Odder tells Kairi.
Sometimes I forget
to be careful.

Kairi paddles in a lazy circle.
One of these days
they will put you in a cage
and I will never see you again.
One of these days
you'll end up at
Highwater for good.

You worry too much, Kairi,
Odder says.

Why
do you get so close
to them?
Kairi asks.

Just curious,
Odder answers.
They helped me once,
don't forget.

Odder submerges her head,
then lifts and shakes it,
and droplets catch the sun.

Highwater

The otters call it "Highwater,"
the aquarium perched
above the edge of the bay.

More land than water,
more air than ocean,
the accommodations are solid,
if you happen to be a
water-dweller.

The staff is first-rate,
the food to die for,
house rules enforced with vigor:
predators kept away from prey,
separated by thick walls of glass.

Not a bad place to stay,
all things considered, although
once you've checked in,
departing can be difficult.

troublemaker

Odder has been
in trouble before.
She has a soft spot for humans—
understandable,
given the way she was raised,
considering all she was taught.

So what if she investigates
a dock or sandbar
from time to time?
So what if she nudges a scuba diver
to say hello?
So what if she tries to leap
onto a kayak or canoe
to better know her story—
is that so wrong?

Yes,
say the other otters,
Kairi, too,
and judging by the way
certain humans

trap and relocate her
to quiet waters away from trouble
whenever she gets too friendly
(eight times and counting),
maybe her friends
have a point.

motherly advice

Odder doesn't remember much
about her mother.
Pups are with their moms
for five months or so,
a year at most,
but Odder wasn't
that lucky.

Still, she does recall
one piece of advice her mother
used to repeat:
Stay away from sharks.
Stay away from humans.
Stay away from all
that you don't understand.

Back then,
Odder didn't know what a human was,
and she'd never seen a shark,
but she got the drift, all right:
Be afraid of the world,
my daughter.

Kairi would have liked
Odder's mother.

fast enough, slow enough

Near the entrance to the slough
the shark hesitates.

He scents the otters, but
doesn't see them clearly,
not yet.
His sight is no match
for his glorious
sense of smell.

They are captivating,
blood-rich,
fast enough to
be a decent challenge,
slow enough
to make an easy meal.

tell me a story

Race you to the Drop?
Odder asks,
glancing at the point
where the slough empties
into the far deeper bay.

I'm tired,
Kairi says.
I don't feel like racing.
Tell me a story instead.

You're just trying
to distract me,
Odder replies.

You know me too well,
says Kairi.

scary stories

Tell me about the Fifty again,
says Kairi,
because it is a scary story,
and scary stories are the best,
at least when the sun is out
and the waters are calm.

Odder shimmies and bounces.
But everyone knows that story,
she says,
and she's right:
The story of the Fifty
is every otter's story.

For a moment,
Kairi seems to be shivering,
her eyes glazed and unseeing.

Kairi?
Odder asks.
Are you all right?

Kairi blinks and
shakes her head.
I'm fine.
Just a little tired.

Odder hesitates.
Kairi hasn't been herself
the past few days.
She's seemed sluggish and
distracted.

You're sure?
Remember when Amaya had
the shaking sickness?

I'm fine,
Kairi says firmly.
The Fifty, please.

Odder dives,
resurfaces,
spirals.

The Fifty,
she begins,
and Kairi clasps her forepaws together
and falls silent.

The Fifty

Once, in times past,
when the ancients lived,
the ocean was filled
with our kind,
Odder says.
But that changed.
Not so very long ago,
there were only fifty of us,
and that was all.

Because of sharks,
Kairi interrupts.

Not really.
Odder twists and twirls.
Not then.

Because of sickness,
Kairi says.

Some.
Odder spins and rolls.

43

But mostly
that came later.

Because why, then?
Kairi asks.

Odder glances at
the faraway kayaker,
now just a drifting dot,
so small he might be
an egret or
a marsh wren.

Because of them,
she says, and
then she plunges
under the waves.

deep dive

A sea otter can stay underwater
for six or seven minutes,
and that is what Odder does.

It's fun

to build suspense.

the end

When Odder blasts
back to air and sun,
her friend is waiting impatiently.
Now tell me the rest,
Kairi demands,
still backfloating.

There is no rest.
Odder somersaults.
There were fifty,
and now there are more,
three thousand, perhaps.

And we are part of the more?
Kairi asks.

All of us, yes.
We all come from
the Fifty.

Odder rubs her nose.
The end.

*I liked it better
the last time you told it,*
Kairi complains.

Stories change,
says Odder
as she zooms past Kairi.
*Now let's find us
some breakfast,
my friend.*

the sighting

The intriguing scent
becomes something more
for the shark.

There they are above him
on the surface,
long, dark silhouettes
with webbed feet
and muscular tails.

He's glimpsed some
before, but never this close.
They are sinuous,
but not eel-sleek.
They don't shimmer in the
way of a mackerel or a ray.

Wouldn't sea lions
be bigger than this?
Maybe these are young sea lions.
Babies, even.

They move surprisingly well,
with a certain elegance.
But they're no match
for him.

One is slower,
and that will be his target.
No reason to expend
extra energy
(although what a feast
two would make).

He feels
the sharp complaint of hunger
and presses on.

the fin

Just a little farther, Odder says,
as the beguiling, wild song
of the bay calls to her.

Kairi is right beside her.
Please, Odder,
she says,
let's go back,
and Odder hears her fear.
We've gone too far.

The sun sparks the waves
as the wind picks up,
and then Odder sees it
and her heart lurches:

gliding,
glimmering,
almost beautiful:
the dorsal fin
of a great white shark.

speed

A few thrusts of the shark's powerful tail,
and he'll have them, easy as that.

Sometimes even he is shocked
by his own speed.

the chase

Odder lets loose
a high-pitched scream,
though Kairi needs no warning.
She is already churning the water,
and Odder sees
the terror in her friend's eyes,
and both otters move
like they have never moved,
but he is on them already.
Odder can feel him
slice the surf
in two, she
can smell his
hunger.

turning back

Odder knows
this is all because of her,
because she is reckless
and wrongheaded
and curious
to a fault.

She hears a strangled cry,
and turns to see
the shark has nipped
her friend's tail,
as the awful stench of blood
blooms in the water.

A full-grown white would have
devoured them both
by now, but
this shark must be young,
inexperienced, or confused.

Kairi is slower,
there is only one

thing to do, and so
Odder twists,
turns back,
passes her
wounded friend,
heading
directly toward those
jagged rows of teeth,
those unfeeling eyes.

confusion

It was just a small bite, but the hint
of blood makes the shark
bold. Some part of him
wonders if he's made a mistake—
the taste, perhaps—
but it's too late, he's pure
muscle and instinct now.

As he moves in for the kill,
he's met with sheer movement,
flipping and twisting,
an eruption of bubbles,
the reek of fear.

It's under him,
behind him,
hitting his flank—
how could it be, but
it is—
it's one of them,
not the one he nipped,

the other—
hurling herself at him.

It's impossible. Never
has he seen anything
move like this.
He tries to focus
on the wounded one,
the slower animal
heading away,
but this other frenzied
thing,
whatever it is,
won't let him be.

trapped

And so he
veers
and there
she is
and his mouth
is open
wide and
waiting and
clamp
snap
gnash
she is
trapped
in his jaws
where
she
belongs.

beyond

Of course she's felt pain,
but this is new,
a black void
beyond hurting,
beyond understanding.

oops

Instantly the shark knows
this is wrong,
all wrong.
His jaws
unlock,
his head
jerks,
his prey
floats free.

It's all fur and bone—
so much hair!—
and not even a hint
of blubber.
A ray would have
been more satisfying,
a rockfish, even.

It's no sea lion,
that's for sure.
The taste is vile,
and he's even lost a

few teeth,
not that it matters.
They pop anew
unbidden.

Still,
what a waste of time,
and good thing
his embarrassing failure
went unwitnessed
by other sharks.

the beach

Perhaps she is swimming,
or perhaps she is dreaming,
because why else would she be
moving like this,
jerkily,
uncertainly,

trailing the smell of
her own impending death?

Somewhere, Kairi
might be calling to her—
this way, this way, this way!
The dizziness
dulls the pain,
makes it seem to belong
to some other animal.

Advice bubbles up,
wisdom gleaned
from older otters—
head for shore,

blood in the water is an invitation,
move as little as necessary,
conserve energy—
and so she
struggles toward
a nearby patch of beach.

Is she imagining it,
or didn't she once find
salvation on
land?

hauled out

"Hauled out," it's called,
and indeed it is a haul,
flopping forty-five pounds
onto solid land when you
are meant for water.

And yet Odder does it,
despite the gaping wound on her belly,
perhaps because she knows
she has done it before,
even as she's drained of blood
and hope.

A gull lands inches
away, preening,
wondering if there
will be something to
gain from such a mess.

Odder blinks. The sun
is so good,
so kind—

how hard it would be to
die at night!

She's not mad
at the gull, doesn't even
blame the shark.

She's seen enough to know
that this is how life is,
and this is how death comes.

retreat

The shark moves on
into deeper waters,
a bit wiser but
still famished,
still wearing the scent
of his victims.

how to rescue a stranded otter

Be wary.
Their river cousins switch
between land and water
like kids at the beach,
but sea otters
prefer the surf.

If you see one where humans tread,
keep your distance.
It might just be an inquisitive sort,
taking a breather,
or it could be sick or hurt
or weakened by hunger.

Everyone will want
to touch the otter—
that fur is the stuff of legend,
and those puppy eyes
pull like a magnet.
Remember, though:
Those jaws are
steel-trap cruel.

Call someone,
someone who knows what to do,
or at least what not to do.
Keep dogs away,
and others who will want
to get too close,
who don't understand
that while you wait for
help to come,
death may be
en route, too.

sounds

Odder's eyes
will not open,
her head will not move,
it is all she can do to breathe
because every breath burns,
but she can, at least,
still listen.

She has created quite a
commotion, it seems.
Voices surge,
people shuffle,
tourists lean in close
and click their cameras.
Gulls cluster and gossip,
enjoying the chaos,
because chaos means
dropped food—
a fry, perhaps,
or even an ice cream cone.
Dogs send out throaty alerts
and a baby howls,

while waves break on the beach,
whispering to Odder
and Odder alone:

Let go, let go, let go.

help arrives

When rescue comes at last,
Odder recognizes
some of the voices,
and her heart clenches
with relief and regret.

She is going back.

She has failed,
though maybe this time
it's already too late, maybe
she will die
before she even gets there.
(She's already been given a chance,
one more than most.)

In any case, she accepts
her fate. If Kairi survives,
there's that,
at least.

The hands are gentle,
the gloves familiar.
Hello, old friend,
someone says,
and though she doesn't
understand the words,
might never understand them,
the music of grief
and disappointment
is not lost
on her.

phantoms

They move her carefully,
but even if she wanted to,
she's too weak to protest.
The bites on her belly,
deep half-moons,
have left her helpless.

The cage smells
antiseptic and unnatural,
but she knows the scent well,
even recalls the rough comfort
of the worn towels.

Phantoms linger here, too—
others like her have
been locked in this cage,
staring through the
metal squares and wondering
if this was their story's end
or its beginning.

the trip

The cage moves in
fits and starts
while time drifts like
a sluggish stream.

For a while the world fades,
until a door opens and
there it is, the scent
she knows as Highwater:
almost ocean,
almost real.

She is back where she began,
where the teaching happened.

Back to the place where
she learned to be an otter.

clinic intake

So few facts:

<u>Intake notes: 3.2 08:10</u>
Age at admit: 3 years 4 months (est.)
Patient: O-156
Previous admit: yes
Sex: F
Species: *E. l. nereis*
Rescue location: Moss Landing State
    Beach, s. end
First call: 07:40—1 stranded, no others
    sighted
Wt: 20.4 kg
Length: 1.2 meters
Dx: lacerations consistent with shark bite

So many questions.

this time

The prognosis is grim,
but still the staff—
they're called "aquarists"—
hope this time all will be well
(they always do),
and sometimes, of course,
they're right.

Things are better
than ten years ago,
five, even. They know
so much more now,
which antibiotics work best,
how to fine-tune the formula,
surgical protocols,
rehab.

And yet understanding the odds,
having done this so many times,
why do their hearts rip open
every time they fail?

Why do they walk
around the clinic for days,
tissues in their pockets, wiping away
tears that keep returning,
relentless as the tides?

surgery

It's an unusual ER,
small but well-equipped,
where the patients come in many forms:
penguins and moon jellies,
sea lions and octopuses,
green turtles and lumpfish.

So much can go wrong
in the ocean:

    run-ins with boats,
              illness from pollution,
                 oil spill exposure,
        entanglement in fishing lines,

ingested plastic trash,
              diseases with too
              many syllables:
        acanthocephalan peritonitis,
              Toxoplasma gondii
              encephalitis.

Of course, shark bites are a problem, too—
more lately, for many reasons.
Could be the warming ocean.
Could be the dwindling kelp forests
where sea otters like to hide.
Could be all the elephant seals
(a favorite meal for sharks)
sharing the neighborhood with otters.

It's all a reminder
to keep hopes

humble.

afterward

The surgery takes hours—
shark teeth are like razors—
but finally Odder is moved to
another small room.
(The aquarium is often
bursting at the seams.)

She will be monitored
day and night, hour by hour,
given fluids and antibiotics,
her respiration checked,
her heart rate noted.

The next days
will be long indeed.
Heads will shake,
worries whispered.

There are so few
of her kind left,
and there's so much more

to learn from her.
That's what they're
all thinking.

delirium

Odder lingers in a twilight place,
not quite awake, not quite asleep,
where memories spin
like waterspouts.

Maybe because the end
is near, she returns
to the beginning of her tale,
when she first drew air as a newborn pup,
three pounds of mewling fur,
so small she could fit
in a shoebox or a sand pail
with room
to spare.

Two

how to be
an otter pup

three years earlier

day 1

When Odder was born
to her mother, Ondine,
she might well have been
an inflatable toy.
Her magical fur
made her buoyant
as a cork.

A pup submerged
will pop back to the surface
like a furry balloon.

a pup's life

Odder was her mother's third pup
(though only the first survived),
and Ondine knew the drill,
knew she would spend
almost every moment
with Odder on her stomach,
clutching her newborn

like a pillow with a heartbeat.

Odder would
drink and sleep,
    sleep and drink,
        drink and sleep—
pups have it easy,
unlike their moms.

(Don't ask where Dad was.
Otter fathers aren't exactly
Parent of the Year
material.)

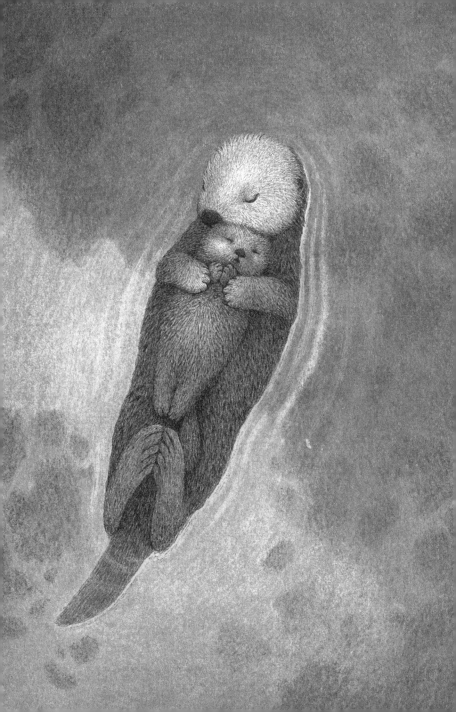

leashed

Ondine could only dive for food
when Odder was safely looped
in long strands of kelp.

Like a leashed puppy
or a reined pony,
it was the only way to be sure
Odder would stay safe
and wave-cradled.

Still, more than a few pups
came unmoored,

drifting away like
stray beach balls.

the otter hair salon

Ondine neglected her own health,
devoting all her energy to
Odder's survival,
and that meant
spending countless hours
at the otter hair salon.

Odder's baby fluff
would soon be replaced
by the warmest fur on earth—
up to a million hairs per square inch,
a miracle of design.
But it's the air bubbles
otters add that keep them
perfectly, impossibly
warm and dry.

Grooming means
fluffing and blowing
    and teasing and separating
and combing and licking
    and tidying and spiffing

and cleaning and cleaning
and cleaning some more.

It isn't vanity.
For otters, it's a matter of
life and death.

The ocean is a
cold place
to call home.

perfect

Otters don't fret much
about what they're called.
When you're all about survival,
names take a back seat.

Still, as the weeks passed,
it became clear that "Odder"
was the perfect choice for
such a squirmy, squeaky pup.
She never calmed,
nursing for a moment,
then raising her downy head to see
if something fun might be
hiding just beyond
the next wave.

day 28

One month in, and Odder was
thriving, though Ondine
could have used a break.

Had a pup ever moved
this constantly?
Even in her sleep,
cuddled close,
Odder was restless,
her front paws dream-busy,
small and soft as
a toddler's mittens.

so much to learn

Ondine was not keeping up
with her own feeding.
She felt tired sometimes,
but at least her milk
was still coming.

Soon Odder would have so much to learn:
when to dive for dinner,
where crabs lurked,
how to eat a sea urchin.
One vital trick
Ondine would be teaching:
using rocks for meal prep.
Such time-savers
when you needed to crack open
a crab or mussel!

For weary Ondine, those lessons
couldn't come fast enough.

tool use

When otters put rocks to work,
humans call it "tool use"
and applaud the ingenuity.

Like chimps and corvids,
octopuses and elephants,
otters have been elevated,
moved up a rung
on the evolutionary ladder,
though every day a new group
seems to join the list of species
that were smarter than
folks thought.

what to fear

Otter pups spend more time
with their moms
than some marine mammals.
Still, they're born with teeth
and ready to swim
as soon as they shed
their life-jacket baby fur.
They grow up much faster
than human children do.

Already Ondine had tried to share
the most important
lesson she could with her pup:
what to fear—
not that she was certain
Odder was listening.

It was never too early
to learn how to stay alive,
and so she reminded Odder
whenever she could:
Stay away from sharks.

Stay away from humans.
Stay away from all
that you don't understand.

It felt wrong,
teaching the little one
who made her cherish life
to be afraid of it.

But that was how things
had to be,
especially with a pup
as heedless
and wild-hearted as Odder.

day 32

One morning Ondine awakened
to unsettled air.
The world smelled strange
and storm-ready.

She secured Odder—extra tightly—
to a favorite stand of kelp.
A quick dive for some urchins
would help Ondine stave off
hunger for a bit.

After the storm, shifting sands
might unearth new meals.

Ondine took one last
glance at her pup.
Odder squealed with
outrage at the abandonment,
as she always did,
while Ondine tried to shake off
her feeling of unease.

It was the dream
she'd had last night, perhaps,
or the coming storm
that had her on edge.

That's all it was.

otter dreams

Humans envy the way
otters sleep on the water,
paws linked,
untroubled as lily pads.

But otters don't just doze.
Like other mammals,
they dream:

flying dreams
where they ride the thermals like hawks,

and shivery nightmares
where all their fur has vanished,

and fretful dreams
where they can't crack open a mussel,
frantic as a student who's forgotten
their locker combination.

the newborn

There was a pup in Ondine's dream,
newborn, needy and squeaking,
though it wasn't Odder.

Odder was there, though—
full-grown, in fact—
and while she wasn't
a mother or a sister or an aunt,
she was somehow important
to the little pup.

Odder kept deep-diving to escape
the pup's demands—
its helplessness frightened her.
When she couldn't hold her breath
a second longer,
she would rocket to the surface,
only to find the pup still there,
still asking for her help.

Dozens of times
    Odder dove,

dozens of times
  she surfaced,
dozens of times
  the pup was waiting.

I can't do it, Odder kept saying.
I don't know how to teach her,

and through it all,
Ondine could only

watch.

just a dream

A dream.

It was just a dream,
Ondine told herself again
as she prepared to dive.

the wind

Her mother was gone,
searching for food, and once more
Odder was forced to wait,
fidgety and annoyed.

The wind was not itself today.
She didn't like the way
it kept bullying the water.

It was awful, each time
her mother left her
alone.
If you asked Odder
(or any otter pup),
life should be nothing
but warmth and milk,
cuddling and play,
on demand,
twenty-four hours a day.

Odder reminded herself that
her mother always returned,

smelling of the baffling underwater world,
and ready again to wrap her pup
in paws instead of kelp.

different

Otters are used to
constant movement.
The tides, egged on by the moon,
never stop, after all.

But this day was different.
The waves grew wild,
flinging Odder
this way and that,
refusing to relent,
while she coughed
and gasped.

It was almost as if
the ocean was angry
at her,
but how
could that be?

rain

Rain came hard
and lightning clawed the sky.
Odder cried out,
but her sounds were lost
in water crashing
and whitecaps boiling.

where is she
she is gone
and what if she is gone
forever?

airborne

Pushed and pulled,
the green and living harness
meant to keep Odder safe
let loose.

No one heard her screams.

When the ocean finally
discarded her,
Odder was no longer afloat
on a watery cushion that
swayed and rocked.

She'd landed somewhere
cold and hard
and everything, everything had

stopped.

waiting

Odder shivered,
choking and crying,
as she listened for her mother's return,
waiting for the clasp of her paws
and the scent of safety.

The rain was just a trickle now,
but where was the ocean?

What was this rough,
unmoving place?

too close

Harsh sounds soon came,
nothing like bird calls, though—
these weren't gulls or terns or
pelicans.

New scents approached, too,
not part of the water world she knew,
and much, much
too close.

shadows

Huge shadows loomed,
cast by tall, tailless animals with
hideous, too-long
forefeet and flippers,
and next came a touch
not her mother's,
not easy and knowing,
though not painful, either,
and the grip tightened,
lifting her off the
solid spot where the ocean
had dropped her.

She tried to fight
her way free,
hissing and snarling
and scrabbling.

But the animal that held her
was strong,
and she
was not.

somewhere new

More movement,
bouncing without waves,
more sounds she'd
never heard before.

She was somewhere new.
The air had changed.
It was cool and dry, not damp
with the ocean's breath.

A soft letting-go happened,
landing her on coarse fur
nothing like her mother's.
Other animals came close,
leaning in.
She tried to struggle,
but couldn't move.
She tried to squeal,
but no one listened.

where is she

After a while,
Odder gave up
trying to fight.
Without the circling waves
and her mother's soothing touch,
all Odder could think was

where is she
where is she
where is she

until finally,
exhausted,
she fell
into a dreamless sleep.

puzzle

The next day, Odder felt stronger.
They wouldn't leave her alone,
the animals,
endlessly feeding and grooming
and measuring and testing,
as if she were a puzzle
they needed to solve.

They kept her in a box
filled with a tiny piece of ocean.
It was long enough
for a little swim,
wide enough
for a twist or spin,
and had a spot above
the water for resting.

At first Odder feared their intrusions,
but when the animals returned
to give her warm food
through a piece of rubber with a hole

(even though it was never as
satisfying as her mother's milk),
Odder was grateful for it.

drowning

When she slept,
Odder fought the ocean
in her dreams,
and always the question
washed over her
until she was sure she would
drown in it:

where is she
where is she
where is she

memories

Odder began to recognize
each of the animals and
even look forward,
just a little,
to their arrival.

It wasn't like
she had a choice.

With every passing hour,
it became harder to recall
her life before this place.

Her mother was
warmth,
Odder reminded herself. She was
food,
and for a while, at least, she was
safety.

But already
the threads of memory

were beginning to fade
and unravel.

chow time

Before long,
Odder could no longer recall
the taste of her mother's milk.
It may have been creamier
or sweeter than the liquid
they brought her every three hours,
but her stomach didn't seem
to know the difference.

When the animals were slow
to arrive, Odder squeaked and complained,
and when her meal finally appeared,
she grunted her approval,
and they made murmuring,
relieved sounds.

It was a conversation,
of a sort.

home away from home

Whatever this strange place was,
it was becoming Odder's home
away from home.

The animals who cared for her
were mystifying.
Their paws had stubby tentacles,
their bodies were practically bald,
and their guttural songs
hurt her ears.

Still, she could not deny
that they were kind,
and that they seemed,
for some unknowable reason,
to want her
to live.

not otters

They weren't so bad, actually,
Odder decided,
these animals with their awkward paws
and confusing noises.

Although nothing they did
was quite right,
it was right enough.

They weren't otters.
But they certainly
were trying to be.

scents

The first time she noticed the scent,
Odder thought she was dreaming.

The animals nursing her back to health
always carried hints of other places with them.
Sometimes it was the brine of salt water.
Sometimes it was the tang of fresh air.
But from time to time she would recognize
a scent that was a little like . . . her.

It was an otter-y smell, rich and reassuring,
but she'd seen no other otters there.

It was a mystery,
but then, everything
about this new life
was a mystery.

swimming lessons

Several times a day, one of the animals
would lift Odder out of her box of water
and carry her to a bigger, round pool,
one with sky and sun above it,
and breezes tinged with salt.
She floated on her back while
they pulled her by her flippers,
carving lazy figure eights.

Now and then Odder would
clutch one of their paws between her own
and the cruise would repeat,
back and forth, back and forth,
as she rode the tiny waves.

Whenever Odder was there,
she knew she belonged to the water,
and it belonged to her.

impossible

When she was happy in the pool,
the animals watched her with care,
clapping their peculiar paws
and revealing their teeth
and making breathy noises,
and always Odder wondered
what it all meant.

They were impossible to decipher,
these big, clumsy creatures.
She would have to watch them carefully
until she knew their ways.
Perhaps the more she understood,
the more she'd be able to
get what she needed from them.

Maybe she'd find her way
back to her life in the wild,
although she was no longer certain
what that might mean.

Would her mother still be
waiting for her, or would
she have moved on to
new places,
new pups?

learning

Even as Odder was learning to
navigate her new world,
her caretakers were learning, too.

This wasn't their first attempt
teaching survival skills to a pup,
and it wouldn't be their last.
Their plan was simple,
on paper, at least:
let 156 explore the ocean
with the help of humans,
until she was ready
to return to the wild alone.

Still, the questions kept them
up at night.

What would 156 need to know
on her journey back to freedom?

Would instinct be enough
to guide her?

How do you turn a helpless, captive pup
into a capable, wild adult?

If only they had a manual, one called
How to Teach an Otter Pup
How to Be an Otter Pup.

It seemed they were going
to have to write it themselves.

mystery

Another question lingered,
one without an easy answer:
What had happened to
156's mother?

They'd searched hard
after 156 was discovered,
but pups and their mothers
were often separated
during violent storms.
Sometimes, with human help,
they could be reunited.
But rescuers couldn't waste time
when a stranded pup
was in danger of dying.

Now here they were yet again,
pretending to be what they
never could be:
otter moms.

keystones

People often asked them:
Why try so hard to save
one little otter?

Look at an old building sometime,
they'd answer.
Look at an arched door,
or maybe a vaulted ceiling.
See that wedge-shaped
topmost stone?

A keystone, that's called,
and without it everything falls,
like a tower of blocks or
a house of cards.

It's the same
with keystone species—
beavers, wolves,
prairie dogs, bees,
desert tortoises, sea otters—

they are nature's glue,
holding habitats together.

Without otters,
sea urchins, purple as a bruise,
gobble kelp forests
until the ocean floor
becomes a barren wasteland.
When enough sea otters
eat enough sea urchins, though,
all is well, and
the arch endures.

It sounds so simple,
but then, so does
stacking blocks into towers,
and we all know how easy it is
to topple those.

fun

And so they kept at it,
pretending to be otters,
doing what they could
to keep 156 alive and happy.

Fortunately, it isn't difficult
to entertain an otter pup, and they had
quite a bag of tricks at their disposal:

shells

                              and algae

    urchins

                              and rocks.

Their motto was simple:
If it belonged to
a wild otter's world,
it was worth a try.

carwash kelp

A few otters at the aquarium
could never return to the wild,
and for them,
another way to play came
from an unexpected source.
A large display tank at the aquarium
had once featured real kelp,
but its otter guests were rowdy,
prone to partying, and so
the management had to improvise.

Instead of living kelp,
strands of rough fabric now drifted—
the kind at the car wash,
sliding over windshields
bathed in bubbles.

The otters could work with it,
they were an adaptable sort.
And at the end of the day,
play was play.

riding the waves

For 156, in her little pool,
the aquarists would sometimes dangle
a frond of real kelp
so she could grab for it, hanging on
while they towed her across the water.

Soon she would understand how
to use kelp as a pup-sitter,
just like her mother.
Soon she would learn to
deep dive,
to open mussels,
to know which predators
to fear.

Such a long to-do list it was,
and they had so little time.

Every hour with humans
meant an hour Odder might become
more attached to them.

And the more attached she grew,
the less willing she might be
to find the freedom she deserved.

changes

For Odder, the shells and rocks
and outdoor pool
were delightful, but just as exciting
was the arrival of solid food.

One day bits of fishy glop
appeared for her consideration.
Odder sniffed the tempting goo,
ever curious, then took a taste.

It was the ocean!
Wasn't this how her mother
had smelled when
she returned from a dive?
Odder could no longer recall
her mother's touch, but this
reminder of life on the waves
was still fresh in her heart.

She was eating the ocean,
and oh my,
how delicious it tasted!

coincidence

Odder liked to take food in her paws
and make the kind of mess
that only determined babies,
faced with a jarful of cooked peas,
can create.

Interesting coincidence:
Once solid food started,
her grooming seemed to take
a whole lot longer.

how to groom an otter pup

How do you groom an otter pup?
Carefully.

To begin with, be afraid.
If you get it wrong, it won't be
just another bad hair day.
If you get it wrong,
she could be lost—
for otters,
temperature is everything.

Be prepared.
You'll need towels,
so many towels,
brushes, little combs,
a hair dryer,
and boundless patience.

Most of all,
be grateful.
Know how lucky you are to care
for this marvel of nature,

to witness her contented sighs
and watch her perfect curl
into slumber.

others

During her first few days at Highwater,
Odder often caught traces of
something beyond her simple life—
scents lingering on the air,
or what sounded like the kind of squeak or hiss
that she herself might make.

Though she would smell curious things
on the animals when they reached for her,
and hear curious things when she lay quietly in
her cage,
every time it happened she told herself
to stop thinking there might be others like her
in this not-quite-home.

What point was there
in hoping?

milestone

Even before she'd shed her baby coat,
Odder's diving lessons began.

At first the aquarists placed
a few cracked clams and mussels
in a sand-filled bowl at the bottom
of her shallow pool,
just a foot or two out of reach.

It seemed to frighten poor 156,
the way they urged her
to explore below the surface.

She didn't understand
that her ears and nostrils
could close at will.

She didn't realize
that the ocean floor
was the ultimate
otter restaurant.

diving

It wasn't easy, diving,
saying farewell to air and light
and forcing herself to head
toward places unknown.

It took all Odder's strength,
and many tries, to talk
her flippers and tail and waterwise body
into doing exactly what they needed to do.

But there it sat, a cracked shell
at the bottom of the pool, and inside that shell
was a luscious clam.

When she finally surfaced,
sat the shell on her chest,
and plucked a tasty snack
from its hiding place,
the animals (her loyal audience)
made sounds that Odder decided
meant they were pleased.

Not that she cared.
She was too busy
slurping down dinner.

the surprise

The next morning it was time
for another diving lesson,
but instead of taking Odder
to the outdoor pool she knew so well,
the animals carried her to
an unfamiliar place.

The smells were enticing
and the room echoed with noise, lots of it—
splashing, bubbling, thumping, squealing.

Were those otter scents?
Otter sounds?

Odder, being Odder,
didn't hesitate a moment.
She plunged into
a huge pool decked out
like a miniature ocean.

The water had smooth, clear sides—
she bumped her nose on invisible walls

before figuring that out—
and it took a while to reach
the faraway sandy bottom
littered with lovely shells.

Small, restless creatures shimmied past—
colorful, but confusing
(fish, she remembered learning from her
mother)—
and fronds of fake kelp swayed
in a slow-motion hula.

But only one thing mattered to Odder,
and as she returned to the surface,
she had her answer.

welcome

Welcome to the tank,
youngster,
said a large, female, silver-tinged
animal.

An otter.

surrounded

Two elderly otters
approached her,
quite determined to sniff and nudge
until they'd assured themselves
she belonged with them.

Despite her curiosity,
Odder felt overwhelmed,
surrounded by such nosy strangers.
She tried to climb out of the tank
to the safety of her little cage,
back to the animals who'd brought her,
but there was no way out,
no ramp or easy exit.

They want you in here,
explained the smaller female.
It's about learning to deep dive.

I know how to dive,
said Odder.

Just wait till you see the ocean,
the otter replied.

just a pup

I was born in the ocean,
Odder said,
circling warily.

I wonder if she's permanent?
asked the other otter.
She had long, thick whiskers
and a notch in one of her flippers.

Poor dear,
said the smaller female,
she looks nervous. Be kind.
She's just a pup, Gracie.
She turned her gaze on Odder.
You're safe with us, little one.

Odder swam backward
until she rammed
the edge of the tank.

They call me Holly,
said the smaller female.
And that's Gracie over there.

We've been here forever,
Holly said.
They decided we weren't fit
for the ocean.

She gave a toss of her silver head.
These days, old and creaky as we are,
they're probably right.

listening

Odder scooted here and there,
keeping her distance,
though she couldn't take her eyes
off the two otters.

And you are?
asked Holly.

It took Odder a moment to
realize she'd been asked a question.
Well, my mother called me "Odder,"
she answered.

But what do they call you here?
Holly asked.
Are you a number or a name?

I'm not sure,
Odder said.

*They only name you
if you're staying for good,*

Gracie said, in a voice that
sounded like she'd
swallowed a fistful of pebbles.
Trust me.
It's better to be a number.

escape

Odder dove and darted,
leaving a frothy trail in her wake.
She had so many questions,
and these old otters
seemed to have plenty of answers.
Still, they made her anxious,
with their talk of names
and numbers
and permanence.

After so much time, shouldn't she be
happier to be
with others like her?
It made no sense.
She longed for the calm of her cage,
her shallow pool, her colorful shells
with their secret treats.

When the big animals finally
allowed her to clamber up a ramp,
she ran to them as if they
were long-lost family,

and she felt, at that moment,
that they were.

the next step

Every day after that,
Odder visited the large tank.
Deep dives soon became
an effortless joy.

While she zipped up and down
the tank, perfecting new moves,
Odder peppered the otters
with questions.

They'd seen pups like her
come and go before, they said.
She was there to learn to
dive deeper than her
usual spot allowed—
the *pup pool*, they called it.

Before long, though,
Odder would probably be promoted,
moved on to the next step:
the ocean.

ready

The very idea of returning
to a life in the wild filled Odder
with a dizzying mix of
yearning and dread.

Are you sure?
she asked them.
Why didn't they send you back?

We couldn't have survived,
Gracie answered,
or so they thought.
There are many reasons.
Sometimes we're too weak,
or too attached to life here.
She paused.
Sometimes we try to return
and the ocean simply spits us back.

What if I'm not ready for the ocean?
Odder asked,

spinning and rolling.

What if the animals are wrong?

humans

Animals?
Gracie repeated,
sounding amused.

Those animals are called humans, my dear,
Holly said.

How do you know?
Odder asked,
toying with a ripply brown shell
she'd found on the tank floor.

If you listen long enough, you learn things,
Gracie said.
Whether you want to or not.

warning

A memory came back to Odder,
a warning shrouded in ocean mist:
Stay away from sharks.
Stay away from humans.
Stay away from all
that you don't understand.

More questions poured out,
one after another:

Should I be afraid of humans?
and
Why would my mother have told me that?
and
What exactly is a shark?

There were sharks in Highwater,
the otters told her,
but they lived in their own tanks
(and, Gracie claimed, weren't nearly
as popular with the visitors as otters).

Her mother was just doing her job,
they said,
teaching Odder to survive.

As for being afraid of humans,
that was a bit more complicated.
The ones here, at least,
were good-hearted.

Beyond these stubborn walls
of impassable water, though,
who could say?

unanswered

Odder never got all the answers
she needed.
After just a few visits,
she graduated
from the tank.
When it came to diving,
she was a superstar.

It was time for the teaching
to get serious.

Before that happened, though,
the animals—the humans—
took her to the room where
they'd first cared for her.

They fussed a while
until they'd attached
a small, clamshell-sized piece
of something flexible
to the webbing
on her left hind flipper.

No matter how fast
she swam or kicked or twisted,
the something would not
come off.

It didn't matter to Odder,
not as long as she could
play in her nonstop way.

tagged

156 was ready.
The aquarists all agreed.

They'd tagged her flipper.
Allowed her to hone her
diving skills in the large tank
(as if 156 needed help).

In any case,
the nagging tick
of an invisible clock
reminded them that time was short
for their beloved little
otter.

outside

On a sun-drenched morning,
two humans, one carrying Odder
in her arms, headed outside.
The assault of smells
was overwhelming.

One of Odder's favorite humans
was barely recognizable,
covered in stretchy new skin
that hid his lumbering, furless body.

His own flippers had been
replaced by larger, imitation ones—
an improvement, to be sure,
but not nearly as nice as her own.

Odder blinked
and there it was:
the place where she was born.
She watched as the water reached out to her,
beckoning with its foamy fingers
before backing away.

Odder squealed and twisted and complained.

What were they waiting for?

This was where she belonged.

open

The human with new skin
and fresh flippers
took Odder in his arms and
stepped into the surf.

Without a pause, she dove.
The water was frigid and murky,
and the bewildering waves
swallowed her down.
The noise was deafening—
did the ocean ever stop talking?—
and Odder realized they'd made
a terrible mistake.

She wasn't
ready for this, not even
close to ready.

panic

She was panicking,
twisting and flipping,
but then there he was, the human,
pretending to be an otter.
His hand brushed against Odder.
He was under the waves,
swept along in the same current,
moving much the same way
she was moving
(though not as gracefully).

Odder's body relaxed into the swells
as she and her almost-otter teacher
dove deeper.
She was no longer afraid
because her teacher didn't seem to be.

She was with someone
who had brought her this far,
someone who seemed to think
she could go even farther.

more lessons

The lessons happened daily,
and always Odder's almost-otter friend,
with his awkward not-quite-flippers, joined her.

Days turned to weeks, and quickly
her fear turned to bliss.
They headed farther and deeper into the water,
and at first she never strayed from his side,
even when she saw wild otters
in the distance.
Over time, though,
Odder grew bolder,
venturing off on her own for a bit.

She explored the kelp forest—
real kelp at last!—where fronds
rode the breathing ocean's rise and fall,
and sea stars and clams lay like gifts
waiting for Odder to open.

She even perfected a new move,
a way to spiral down

to the sandy floor in style:
a giddy, pinwheeling
tornado.

Why simply dive
when she could dazzle?

return

Always when it was time to
leave the water behind,
Odder wondered why.

Why couldn't the two of them
stay there forever?
Why did they have to leave
this endless playground
for a place so plain and small?
Why bother with kelp clippings
when a whole forest of real kelp awaited?

Still, Odder allowed him to take her
back to Highwater again and again.
He was her teacher,
her safe harbor.

The quick-tempered bay didn't care
if she lived or died.

Odder's dream

One night after a perfect day of diving,
Odder dreamed of a pup,
a newborn female.
She'd had dreams about pups before,
but this one was different,
haunting and too real.
The tiny pup was trapped in knots of kelp,
unable to free herself, and
Odder was the only one who could hear her
desperate calls for help.

Odder tried everything,
tearing through the kelp with her teeth,
her claws, her body,
but nothing she did made any difference.

She awoke, trembling,
the pup's cries still echoing
in her mind.

It was just a dream,
she told herself.

Just a dream.

the wild otters

The next morning, the bay was sullen,
as quiet as she'd ever seen it,
flat and gray.
Diving—as always, with her otter-teacher—
was almost too easy:
Urchins were begging to be claimed,
and swimming was as effortless
as breathing.

After surfacing a few times,
Odder noticed movement
on the horizon.
Two otters swimming,
that's all it was. She'd seen
others, of course—
had even played with a few—
and while they always intrigued her,
she'd never felt moved to stay with them.

But this time, Odder was mesmerized
by the way they splashed and cavorted.
She couldn't stop watching their

spins and somersaults,
almost (but not quite)
as impressive as her own.

They could have been her.
They were her.

the leaving

It was nothing new,
seeing those otters,
so why did it feel different this time?
She was still Odder,
tied by invisible threads
to her human caretakers.

Maybe it was the dream she'd had.

Maybe it was the calm, glassy water,
inviting her to take a chance.

Maybe it was the exuberant way
the otters owned the waves—
the way she loved to move.

Maybe it was simply time.

Her otter-teacher surfaced.
She looked at him fondly,
the human who knew so little

about how to be an otter,
and yet had taught her so much.

He and the other humans
had saved her from death.
She knew in her heart that
she owed them everything,
the same way she knew she had to
swim away now,
this very moment,
before she changed her mind.

how to say goodbye to an otter

Be hopeful.
She's been tagged with ID,
and you'll be checking on her
constantly. Besides, she's
a prodigy in the water.

Know you've taught her well,
that she is ready for this moment,
that there is never a perfect time
to let go of the ones we love.

See that gleaming head
and spinning body,
watch her submerge
into a world where you
will never belong.

Imagine that dive of hers,
that hypnotizing cyclone
of fur and bubbles,
and smile through
your joyful tears.

Three

otter #209

the present

recovery

After almost three years of freedom,
Odder again lies in a cage at Highwater.
Eight days have passed
since the shark attack.

Her first time here, she'd been a helpless pup.
Now she's a helpless adult,
pieced back together by the same humans
who'd once fed her formula every three hours
and groomed her fluffy coat like
doting otter moms.

Her whole body throbs or aches or itches.
The humans won't let her lick her wounds,
though every fiber of her being tells her
that's exactly what she needs to do.
She's back in her old pup pool,
and they can't seem to stop
jabbing and jostling her.

Still, she knows it's wise
to tolerate their meddling.

That much, at least,
she's learned the hard way.

regret

As bad as the discomfort is,
the regret is worse.

How could she have been so reckless,
venturing so far into the bay?
How could she have put herself,
and poor Kairi, at risk?
Had her mother's warnings
meant nothing?

Odder promises herself that
when she returns to the water
she will be different,
cautious and sensible and
grown-up and boring.
She won't venture too far,
won't long for those
mouthwatering bay crabs,
won't spend every moment
working on yet another
thrilling move.

She will stop being Odder.

looking

As she slowly recovers,
memories of her time in the wild
fill Odder's long days.

After she'd left her otter-teacher behind
(she'd thought of it as a daring escape,
but of course there was no way
he could keep her from departing),
it seemed she spent
every waking moment searching—
for what, she wasn't always sure.

In a way, it didn't matter.
Searching meant swimming,
and swimming meant play,
and play was her purpose.

At first, she looked for her mother,
but no one seemed to know
what had happened to her.
Mothers moved on.
That was the way of things.

She searched for friends,
and soon she found Kairi and others
to keep her company.
Sometimes they would
float together, paws entwined,
two dozen otters or more,
a comforting tangle of whiskers and tails.

She searched for sharks,
saw a few, and knew to
keep her distance.

She searched for food,
always ready to grab another morsel.
It's hard to play when
your stomach has other ideas.

And even though she'd left
them behind,
she could never seem
to stop searching for more humans,
no matter how hard
she tried.

visits

Odder's former caretakers were
on the lookout for her, too.
To her surprise, she often
caught sight of them
in a ridiculous puttering boat,
watching her
watching them.
(No doubt they needed the boat
because they were such
lousy swimmers.)

Now and then, when she
tailed a diver or visited a kayaker
or ventured too close to a curious tourist,
her old friends would appear
with a net and a cage.

Eventually they would manage
to catch her, and,
with heavy sighs and rolled eyes,
move her away to an area

with more otters
and fewer humans.

It was a pointless game,
one she didn't understand,
but like any devoted student,
she was always delighted
to touch base
with her former teachers.

mistake

She loved her time of freedom,
though there were hungry days
and lonely ones,
and Odder constantly reminds herself
that she would still be
whipping through whitecaps,
if only she'd been more careful.

One shark.
One mistake.

That's all it takes
to change your life forever
when the ocean is your home.

rehab

At last the humans decide
Odder is healthy enough
to play in the larger rooftop pool,
the one with sky and sun
and bright, clean air,
but her body refuses to behave
the way she wants it to.
She's stiff and fumbling,
and every move feels
as graceless as a human's.

Still, it's water,
beautiful water,
and that's all that matters.

stronger

One morning, Odder is
moved to someplace new.

As the humans carry her,
Odder samples the air. The otter tank!
There's another vague scent, too,
one that makes her heart quicken,
but only after she's splashed into the water
can she ask Gracie and Holly:
Is there another otter here?
An otter named Kairi?

catching up

Hello to you, too,
says Holly, as she and Gracie
swirl around Odder,
examining her scars
and sniffing her head.

Tell us all about it,
Gracie urges,
and Holly says, not unkindly,

*You're moving as slowly
as we are, my girl.*

Odder stays silent
so the old otters will calm.
I will tell you the whole story,
she finally says.
*But first you have to answer me:
Is there another otter here?*

Gracie paws at an ear.
They call her Twyla,

she said. *But I think her*
wild name was Kairi.

Kairi. Here.

Where is she?
Odder demands.
And why is she here?
Is she hurt?
She remembers Kairi's nipped tail
and the horrible smell of blood.
Is it because of a shark bite?

No, dear,
Holly replies.
She has the shaking sickness,
but the humans are making it better.

Odder dives and circles
to calm herself. When she
emerges, she asks,
If Kairi is better, then why
isn't she here with you?

The pup,
Gracie answers,
as if it's obvious.
The one that died.

Twyla

They tell Odder the story then,
how an otter the humans called "Twyla"
was found beached, shuddering
with the sickness that so many otters
seemed to have these days.
No one realized that she would soon
give birth to a pup.

How she joined the tank not
long ago, and how they'd
had to tell her the truth:
When the humans name you,
it means you are here to stay
for good.

How one day she gave birth
to a stillborn pup
and held its lifeless body,
hugging it close for hours.

How the humans
had slowly, gently

removed her and the pup
from the tank.

Where she was now,
no one knew.

back in the tank

While it's good to be out of the pup pool
and see the two old otters again,
knowing what Kairi has gone through
haunts Odder's return to the tank.

It helps a little to know it's not
Odder's fault that Kairi is here—
but only a little.
It hurts, not being able to reassure
her old friend, to call her *silly minnow*
and do daredevil tricks until
worrywart Kairi
is secretly amused.

If she finds Kairi here,
Odder will promise
her that all will be well.
She'll make up a riveting story
with a splendid ending,
one where Kairi roams free in the slough
with a healthy, newborn pup.
Odder will be in the story, too—

she'll be the doting auntie
who teaches the pup
all her best moves.

No matter how many times Odder
practices the tale, though,
she knows it's just a lie
without an ending.

wrong

Days pass, and everything is wrong.
There's no sign of Kairi,
and there's no sign
of the old Odder, either.

She's slowly healing, but she simply
can't move the way she used to.
Her playful, mischievous self
has vanished. The shark attack
shadows her the way a stubborn cloud
can steal the sun.

The elderly otters try to encourage her,
but nothing helps. She's beginning to
wonder if she'll ever leave this place.
Maybe she's meant to grow old here,
like the others.

Not long ago, Gracie reminded her
that wild otters who spend
too much time near humans
are sometimes brought to Highwater

for their own safety.
Gracie was one of those curious types,
she admitted.

Odder thought back to all
the kayakers and divers,
boaters and tourists
she'd investigated
over the years.
I was like that, too,
she said softly.

Still, she knows that even if she'd listened
to her mother's warnings
and stayed far away from humans,
even if she'd evaded the shark,
there were plenty of other reasons
she might have ended up here at Highwater.

Look at Kairi, timid and vigilant.
She'd done everything right,
and it hadn't mattered in the least.

exam

The aquarists want Odder to exercise.
They cajole and implore,
dangling treats just out of reach,
but she ignores them.

She is eating little, diving even less,
so they take her to the exam room,
check her vitals, X-ray her belly,
manipulate her paws and flippers,
and when she is passive and silent,
they worry. Where is the
rambunctious pup
they used to know?

Could she possibly sense, somehow,
the heartbreaking decision
they've finally reached?

No.
Of course not.

It's the right thing to do,
and they know it,
given her injuries
and her long history of
risky encounters with people.
But the notion that she'll never
again float in the slough,
linked, like a vital puzzle piece,
to other otters
(a "raft," it's called),
is hard to accept.

They can't help feeling,
despite everything they've done,

that they've let
their dear friend down.

human noise

It's Gracie who notices first.

She's spent years hearing human noise,
deciphering what she can.
When sounds are repeated,
it's a sign that something matters
(to the humans, anyway).

Many noises end with a food reward,
and that's reason enough
to listen with care:
"Gracie" means her.
"Good girl" means a treat.
"Come" means swim to the edge of the tank.
"Wait" means prepare to be annoyed.

It's only because she's had so much practice
that Gracie takes note of the sound
humans have begun using
whenever Odder's near:
"Jazz."

"Good girl, Jazz," they say.
"Come, Jazz."
"Wait, Jazz."

The humans, she fears,
have given her young friend
a name.

never

For two days, Gracie waits.
She doesn't have the heart to tell Odder
that she, like the rest of them,
will never be leaving.

Jazz

She's not surprised, not really.
For Odder, it feels like that day
of the shark attack, when she
lay waiting to die.

It's a relief, giving up
and accepting the inevitable.

Hope can be
exhausting.

spared

As the days blur together,
a calm acceptance sets in.
Truth is, it feels only fair,
sharing the fate of her friends.
Why should Odder
be any different?

And honestly, this life at Highwater
isn't so bad, is it?
She's safe and cared for,
loved, it seems, by
her human caretakers.

Most importantly,
she'll be forever spared
the dark, determined threats
of ocean life.

no sign

Sometimes Odder thinks
she catches Kairi's scent in the air,
but there's been no sign of her old friend
since the pup's death.
Every now and then other intriguing smells
waft past, and Odder will
look to the elderly otters to
see if they, too, have noticed anything.

But their noses don't work
as well as they used to,
and Odder tells herself that
she's probably just imagining things.
She's good at that,
it appears.

absurd

This afternoon two of the humans
come calling for her:
"Jazz! Come, Jazz!"

They tap on the edge of the tank,
and she ignores them to make it clear
she's not interested.
But when a shred of crabmeat appears,
Odder meanders over to accept the treat
between her paws.

She glances at the humans
and is surprised to see that one
has covered herself in a confounding way.
(Humans are always wearing
things to hide their lack of fur, of course,
but this new effort is startling.)
From the neck down, the human is
sheathed in something
thick and loose and dark
that hides her appendages,

while her head is completely covered
by a black boxlike object.

Even by human standards
(which is saying something),
she looks foolish.

Not for the first time,
Odder is grateful for her
luxurious fur.
Human bodies seem to
offer plenty of opportunities
for humiliation.

up to something

Another piece of crab, another
instruction:
"Cage, Jazz. Cage."

Clearly, they want her to climb up a ramp
and enter the small cage that awaits.
But that cage means a visit to the exam room
where humans like to prod and measure her,
and she is fine, thank you very much.

More crab is offered, and when Odder
still won't leave the tank,
they resort to trapping her
in a net.

It's an unusual move,
and a bit embarrassing,
but then, she's being
unusually stubborn.
Odder hisses and screeches
to show her displeasure.

They are up to something,
that much is clear.

knowing

A few minutes later,
they approach the rooftop where
her old pup pool is located,
and even before the door creaks open,
Odder knows with absolute certainty,
as surely as she
knows how to play:

Kairi is here.

back to the pup pool

Odder squeals and chirps and wiggles.
The boxhead human carries
her cage toward a pool,
while the other human stays behind.
As soon as the cage door opens,
Odder leaps into the water
with an impressive splash.

Kairi is in a small pool nearby,
close enough for Odder
to catch a glimpse of her friend.

Kairi looks well. Her fur gleams,
and she's gained some weight.
She is floating on her back,
hugging a little toy to her chest,
moving in her slow, deliberate
Kairi way.

Kairi!
Odder darts back and forth.
I've missed you!

she cries,
but her old friend is silent.

Kairi?
Odder repeats,
even louder.

Hello, Odder,
Kairi whispers at last.
I've missed you, too,
my friend.

bribes

Before she leaves, the boxhead human
praises Odder with reassuring noises.
She even gives Odder floaty toys
and ice cubes filled with
tempting shreds of crab.

But Odder isn't so easily bought off.
Why has she been brought to her old pup pool?
Maybe she's here to keep Kairi
company, but if that's the case,
why aren't they sharing the same pool?

Normally, Odder would be furious,
but something else
has caught her attention,
something fascinating.

ball of fluff

When Odder rushes
to the edge of the pool
and lifts her head just so,
she can see them both clearly.

Kairi isn't holding
a toy.

She's holding
an unbearably tiny pup,
a ball of fluff so small
that Odder wonders
if it's really an otter at all.

I thought . . .
Odder begins.
I thought your pup . . .

maybe

She did,
Kairi answers simply.
She died.

I'm so sorry,
Odder whispers.
It happens sometimes,
they say.

But then—
Kairi nudges the little one
cuddled on her chest—
then they brought me this pup.
I don't know how, or why, Odder.
Maybe he was . . .
Kairi trails off.

Maybe he was all alone,
says Odder.
The way I was.

small

The pup makes a soft squeak,
and Kairi nuzzles him.

How do you know
what to do?
Odder asks.

I just . . . do,
says Kairi, and she looks
as mystified as Odder.

Odder stares for a while,
barely moving.
The pup looks utterly safe
in Kairi's paws,
sheltered from all the world's
unkindness.

Could we ever have been this small?
Kairi asks.

No,
says Odder, trying
to shake off the sudden sadness
dragging her down
like a whirlpool.
Never.

echoes

Odder makes a hard dive,
remembering too late
how shallow the pup pool is.
She bumps her head, then
circles the pool uneasily.

Had she ever been held that way
by her own mother,
with such tenderness?
Had she ever had the chance to be
so protected and loved?

All Odder can recall
from those early days
is a question that still
echoes in her dreams:

where is she
where is she
where is she

sorry

That night, the full moon swims
past the stars, glowing like a sea jelly,
while Odder watches its journey.

From time to time the pup
squeaks or whimpers or whines,
and Kairi soothes him with
coos and pats.

The old otters told me you were sick,
Odder says, after a long silence.

The shaking sickness, yes,
says Kairi.
Like Amaya and the others.

I'm sorry,
says Odder,
paddling listlessly.

The humans made me better,

Kairi says.
It's not so bad these days.

Odder twirls a toy
between her paws.
Kairi?
she whispers.

Yes?

I'm sorry about what happened.
About how I put you in danger.

Odder pauses,
waiting for her friend's
harsh reply.

She hears Kairi
whispering to the pup.

Kairi?
Odder asks.

It was nothing,
Kairi says.
Nothing at all,
you silly minnow.

boxheads

The humans continue to visit
at precise intervals, day and night,
always dressed in their
inexplicable gear.

They pause to say hello to Odder,
giving her treats and attention,
but they seem obsessed
with Kairi and the pup.

When they remove him
from her grasp, however briefly,
his screams of outrage,
and Kairi's anxious groans,
send Odder underwater
to drown out the sounds.

bye, Jazz

When the humans leave,
they make the noises
Gracie has taught
Odder to recognize:
"Bye, Jazz."
"Bye, Twyla."

The door clicks shut.
Those sounds are names,
Odder says.
Our new names.

I know,
Kairi answers.
The old otters told me
what that means.

The pup makes a
sweet, whistling sound.

What about him?

Odder asks.
What do you call him?

Just "pup,"
Kairi answers,
slowly crossing the pool.
I think I'm afraid to name him.
It feels like bad luck.

Do you think—
Odder hesitates.
Do you think they'll name him,
the way they've named us?

I hope not,
Kairi says.
I want him to be free.

why

Odder peers over the pool's edge.
Kairi and the pup might as well be
a single animal. It's hard to tell where one
begins and the other ends.

Why do you want him to be free?
Odder presses.
Do you really want him to face
what we faced?
You were so sick.
And the shark nearly
got us both.

Kairi is silent.

Remember the story of the Fifty?
Odder asks.
Why do you think there were only
fifty of us left in our waters?
The humans were killing us for our fur,
Kairi.

But things are different now,
Kairi says.

It's Odder's turn to fall silent.
He's safe here, at least,
she finally says.

That doesn't sound like you, Odder,
Kairi says.

Odder considers for a moment.
Maybe,
she says,
*that's because I'm not really
Odder anymore. I'm Jazz.*

the answer

Another day passes,
and the boxhead humans keep coming,
gathering to coo about the pup.
They seem pleased with Kairi,
their voices high-pitched and animated,
like shorebirds at dawn.

They still give Odder plenty
of toys and treats, but she feels like
an afterthought. Why do they
insist on keeping her here,
when the big otter tank awaits?
What is the point?

Early the next morning,
two boxheads arrive,
but instead of going straight
to Kairi, they approach Odder,
and at last,
whether she wants it or not,
she has the answer
to her question.

day 1 with pup

One of the boxheads clutches
a towel in her arms,
covering something
squirming and squealing,
and of course Odder
knows what it is,
she can smell it,
she can see its flippers
and a hint of its whiskers,
and still,
when they open the towel
and ever so gently
place the pup
in the pool,

for a moment,
Odder stops
breathing.

the new addition

This pup is bigger than the one
Kairi is caring for, and louder—
her shrill complaints
hurt Odder's ears.
She's clumsy and sputtering,
as if she's new to the water,
and scrawny as well.
Her eyes, too large for the rest of her,
gleam like sea stones
as they lock on Odder.

The humans are watching
Odder—at least, it seems
like they are. It's hard to
tell with their boxheads,
but there's an air of
expectation in the room,
as if they're waiting for her
to perform a task so they
can deliver a treat.

The pup, with great effort,
splashes over
to a tangle of kelp fronds
and does her best
to hide.

For her part, Odder dives
to the far side of the tank.

So this is why
they brought Odder here:
to be another Kairi.
Well, she'll never be like her friend.
She's not calm and kind
and patient and careful.
She nearly got
them both killed, after all.
She may not be Odder anymore.
But she's definitely not Kairi, either.

all day long

All day long,
the humans hover.

All day long,
the pup squeals.

All day long,
Odder ignores her.

reprieve

In the evening,
one of the boxheads
catches the pup in a net,
and Odder is finally
free to roam the tank
in peace.

I wonder where they're taking her,
says Kairi.
It's the first thing
she's said all day.

I don't know,
Odder replies.
*I'm just glad to have
my pool back.*

Odder dips
and dives and twirls
for a while.

What was she like?
Kairi asks when Odder pauses
to loll in the kelp.

She was noisy,
Odder says.
And clumsy.
And she smelled funny.

Like all pups, then,
Kairi says.

After retrieving some food—
she hadn't realized how hungry
she was—Odder asks,
What was I supposed
to do with her?

Kairi's pup makes a noise,
half-purr, half-peep.

Well, what did the humans do with you,
Kairi asks,

when you were brought here
as a pup?

I don't know,
Odder says.
It's hard to remember.
I suppose . . .
She slips underwater to grab a clam,
then surfaces.

You suppose what?
Kairi presses.

I suppose you could say,
Odder replies,
that they taught me how
to be an otter.

Exactly,
says Kairi.

day 2 with pup

The pup returns.
She hides in the strands of kelp.

All day long,
the humans hover.

Now and then,
the pup squeals.

All day long,
Odder ignores her.

day 3 with pup

The pup returns.
She hides in the kelp.

All day long,
the humans hover.

The pup barely
makes a sound.

All day long,
Odder ignores her.

day 4 with pup

The pup returns.
She hides in the kelp.

All day long,
the humans hover.

The pup is silent.

At the end of the day,
Odder swims over
to see if the pup
is still alive.

She is.

meeting

The next morning, before
they return the pup (she's #209)
to Jazz's tank, the aquarists hold a meeting.
Is there something else they can do
to get Jazz to accept the pup
so in need of her help?

Maybe not.
Maybe they're asking
too much of her.

They'd tried this once before,
after all, and it hadn't worked.
Twyla is their first success story,
and it's still quite early. Maybe because
she'd just given birth, bonding
came more easily for her.

Is there any reason to expect
feisty, unpredictable Jazz
to react the same way?

It almost seems unfair.
She's already gone
through so much.

Darth Vader

Still, though it's an incredible long shot,
what if this works? What if,
instead of humans teaching
abandoned pups how to be otters,
they can recruit *actual* otters—
otters who could no longer survive
in the wild? Otters like Twyla and Jazz?

The aquarists don their strange costumes,
the ones they call their "Darth Vader" look.
It's harder to move, covered
in a thick black poncho, gloves,
and a welder's helmet,
but it's also harder for the pups

to recognize humans,
make eye contact,
and bond.

It's simple, and yet so complicated:
If 217 and 209 are going to survive
in the wild, they need to understand
that they are otters,
not agile, charming,
furry humans.

another dream

Odder awakens from
another dream
about a pup.

The pup is drowning.

And Odder lets her drown.

talking

Odder cries out,
and Kairi calls,
Odder, are you all right?

Bad dream,
says Odder,
shaking her head.
That's all.

They'll be bringing the pup soon,
Kairi says,
as if Odder
needs reminding.

I'm hoping they've given up,
says Odder.

Kairi doesn't say anything
for a long while.
What about the pup?
she finally asks.

What about her?
Odder says.

She takes a deep breath.
I'm not like you, Kairi.
I get in trouble. I don't listen.
I nearly got you killed.
I don't know how to
take care of that pup.
I barely know how to
take care of myself.

You know how to play,
says Kairi.

day 5 with pup

The pup returns.
She hides in the kelp.

All day long,
the humans hover.

The pup is silent.

At the end of the day,
Odder swims over.
She gives the pup a nose-tap,
a barely there touch.

The pup whimpers.

She is still alive.

pathetic

Odder reaches out
a paw.
The pup's eyes
go wide.
She squeals and
tries to paddle away,
but her flippers tangle
in pieces of kelp.

She twists and turns,
but she can't free herself.
Clearly, she has
no idea how to dive.

Odder pulls away,
stunned.
She was never this
helpless, was she?
This weak
and needy?

She glances at the boxheads,
watching her and the pup,
and remembers the first time
the humans tried to teach her
to dive.

True, they'd understood
the mechanics—the how—
but there was no way they
could know the why:
the shocking, miraculous
joy of it all.

The pup twists harder.
For a moment,
her head is underwater.
She emerges,
horrified at how
wet her face is,
frantically rubbing her nose
with her tiny paws,
squeaking with
fear and frustration.

The boxheads move
toward the tank with their net,
ready to rescue
the poor pup.

purpose

Odder can't stand it
any longer.

No otter should be this
terrified of the water.

Water means play,
and play is their purpose.

calming

Odder dives underneath the pup
and pushes her past the
knot of kelp.

The pup writhes and squeals,
but Odder performs a roll,
slipping beneath the pup,
then rises,
floating on her back,
clutching the soft mound
of fur close,
until the little pup
finally relaxes.

Back and forth
across the pool
Odder moves,
gliding,
cradling,
calming.

whispers

The humans are making
happy noises,
and so is Kairi,
but Odder isn't paying
attention, because
she is whispering
to the pup clinging
to her as if Odder means
the difference between life
and death.

Little one,
she says,
if I am going to be
your otter-teacher,
let's get one thing
straight.

I will teach you how to
dive for mussels,
how to open clams,
how to anchor yourself

with kelp when you sleep.
And yes, like my mother,
I will teach you
to fear sharks
and avoid humans,
because, dear one,
I must.

The pup taps Odder's
nose with her paw
and makes a purring sound.

Odder thinks of her mother,
of her warnings about the world,
her fretting and worrying,
and for the first time,
she understands.

Most of all,
says Odder,
I am going to teach you
how to play,
silly minnow.

Again the pup purrs.

I've got some moves,
Odder says,
you're not going
to believe,
and suddenly she
cannot wait for
tomorrow.

There is so much
this little pup
needs to know.

coda

six months later

how to say goodbye to an otter (otter version)

Be proud.
After long months,
know you've done your best,
that *teaching* and *loving*
are different words
for the same thing.

Be hopeful.
Imagine them
as the cages open,
as they leap into
the wild water
to use what you have shared,
to take chances and
make mistakes,
to be lonely sometimes,
and lost,

but always,
to know that

the world is not
meant to be feared,

and that water,
beautiful water,
will always mean
play.

Glossary

<u>abalone:</u> an edible shellfish whose shell features a
shiny layer called "mother-of-pearl"

<u>acanthocephalan peritonitis:</u> a parasitic infection
that can cause death in sea otters

<u>antibiotics:</u> drugs that can cure many bacterial
illnesses

<u>bay:</u> a small body of water partially surrounded by
land and connected to a larger body of water

<u>blubber:</u> a thick layer of fat found under the skin

<u>clam:</u> a small, edible shellfish

<u>eelgrass:</u> an underwater plant providing food and
habitat for many species

<u>great white shark:</u> the world's largest known
predatory fish

<u>hauling out:</u> leaving water to go ashore

<u>invertebrate:</u> an animal without a spine

<u>kelp:</u> brown seaweed found in cold coastal waters

keystone species: a species that is vitally important to
    the health of an ecosystem

mussel: an edible sea creature with a dark shell

parasite: a small creature that lives on or in another
    animal and causes disease

predator: an animal that kills and eats other animals

prey: an animal that is hunted for food

raft: a group of otters floating together

rehab: the process of helping someone or something
    that is sick or injured return to wellness (short
    for "rehabilitation")

river otter: otters found near rivers, lakes, streams,
    and freshwater wetlands, with smaller bodies and
    shorter fur than sea otters

sea star: an ocean invertebrate with five or more arms
    (often called a "starfish")

sea urchin: a spiny marine invertebrate, usually
    globe-shaped

slough: a wetland area, usually connected to a larger
    body of water

southern sea otter: the smallest marine mammal in
    North America, once hunted to near-extinction
    for its fur

surrogate: a substitute or stand-in

tagging: the process of attaching identification, uniquely colored and numbered, used by scientists and environmentalists to track many kinds of mammals and birds

Toxoplasma gondii encephalitis: illness caused by a parasite that can result in seizures ("shaking sickness") and death; often transmitted to otters through the waste matter from wild or domestic cats

vitals: important measures of health, including temperature, blood pressure, pulse rate, and respiratory rate (also "vital signs")

Author's Note

"Fiction is the lie that tells the truth, after all," author Neil Gaiman once said, and this novel in free verse is, in fact, inspired by true—and truly impressive—events.

All the otters in this story are loosely based on real otters who've been fortunate enough to be cared for by the remarkable staff of the Monterey Bay Aquarium in Monterey, California. I've chosen to reimagine their stories by combining elements and merging time lines, but if you're interested in the history of an individual animal, please check out the aquarium's website, where you can learn much more (montereybayaquarium.org).

To begin with: Odder (aka "Jazz").

Odder's fictional backstory blends pieces of the lives of two actual Monterey Bay Aquarium SORAC (Sea Otter

Research and Conservation) program otters: Joy and Selka. In 1998, Joy was found stranded when she was just a few days old. This was still early in the program, when scientists were attempting to teach Otter 101 to pups, performing the role of full-time otter moms. That included swimming with young otters in the bay to encourage their development of foraging skills and to provide opportunities for frolicking among wild sea otters. At five months of age, Joy finished her training and swam off. For three years, she continued to revisit her relationship with humans by leaping onto kayaks and docks, until she was finally declared "non-releasable" by the U.S. Fish and Wildlife Service. After reacclimating to aquarium life, she raised sixteen orphan pups.

Selka's story is somewhat different. She, too, was found alone as a week-old pup and cared for at the aquarium. She remained there for almost a year, but only eight weeks after she was finally released, she was found with severe shark bite injuries. Once again, she was cared for at the aquarium, but her eventual return to the wild was marred by continuing health problems. She was declared non-releasable, like Joy, and spent some time at Long Marine Laboratory with otter researchers before returning to the aquarium in 2016 to became a permanent resident and surrogate mom.

As for Kairi (aka "Twyla"), her life echoes that of Toola, the first successful surrogate mother at the aquarium, who lived from about 1996 to 2012. Toola was found stranded, stricken with toxoplasmosis, and later gave birth to a stillborn pup. As it happened, a newborn pup had been found abandoned at almost the same moment, and aquarists were able to place the pup with Toola.

Soon after that, Joy was paired with another stranded pup once he was weaned and could eat solid food. No one was certain what would happen. Unlike Toola, Joy hadn't just given birth. But Joy proved to be a natural teacher and a loving surrogate mom.

Many of the pups raised by Joy, Selka, and Toola have gone on to thrive in the wild, raising their own pups and contributing to the health of Elkhorn Slough and Monterey Bay.

Gracie and Holly were inspired by Goldie and Hailey, two beloved otters at the aquarium who lived to ripe old ages.

Eliminating the element of human bonding has been crucial to positive outcomes for the surrogacy program. The use of Darth Vader disguises—welder's helmets and dark ponchos—proved to be an additional way to ensure that otter pups wouldn't bond with humans during their time at the aquarium. And with real otters as teachers, it was no longer necessary for aquarists to take otters on diving excursions, like the one where Joy escaped.

Odder's story of "the Fifty" refers to the miraculous discovery of around fifty sea otters in the waters near Big Sur in California in 1938. By that time, fur traders and hunters had killed off most of the sea otter population during what is referred to as the California Fur Rush. Over time, with the help of conservation efforts and legislation, that tiny population has grown to about three thousand otters living in a much smaller piece of their original range.

The IUCN (International Union for Conservation of Nature) maintains a list of endangered species, often called the Red List. Sea otters are currently listed as endangered.

The Monterey Bay Aquarium has had amazing success saving stranded and orphaned baby otters, and its work is being studied and replicated all over the world. If you are ever in California, it's absolutely worth a visit.

The world is lucky indeed to have the folks at the MBA Sea Otter Rescue and Conservation program working tirelessly to heal the ocean, one otter at a time.

An otter with her pup.

Spend an hour watching otters frolic, and you'll come away forever changed.

Acknowledgments

Nobody makes books with more love and care than the team at Feiwel and Friends/Macmillan, and I'm so grateful to be a part of their family. Huge thanks go to Liz Szabla, my editor, whose insight and talent is matched by her kindness. Other amazing members of the team include:

- Jean Feiwel, publisher
- Rich Deas, senior creative director
- Helen Seachrist, senior production editor
- Starr Baer, copy editor
- the MCPG marketing and publicity folks, especially Chantal Gersch, Mary Van Akin, and Elysse Villalobos
- Jennifer Edwards and the incomparable sales force

I'm also deeply grateful to:

-  the remarkable Charles Santoso, for *Odder*'s beautiful cover and interior illustrations
- Elena Giovinazzo, my wonderful agent at Pippin Properties, for her wisdom and advocacy
- Mary Cate Stevenson and Noah Nofz at Two Cats Communications for . . . well, a little bit of everything
- Gennifer Choldenko, who is equally talented at friendship and at writing
- the Rogue Colors, always there for solace and a good laugh
- my friends and family, who know a whole lot more about otters than they did a year ago
- and book people of all stripes, especially booksellers, teachers, and librarians: heroes always, but especially these days

For anyone interested in learning more about sea otters, I highly recommend starting with Todd McLeish's entertaining and fascinating book, *Return of the Sea Otter*, for an in-depth look at the history and hopes surrounding these captivating creatures.

While I am deeply indebted to the staff members of the Monterey Bay Aquarium for their help with my research, any mistakes are entirely my responsibility.

Special thanks go to Teri Nicholson, senior research biologist at Monterey Bay Aquarium, and to Sandrine Hazan, stranding and rehabilitation manager—sea otters, for their truly helpful input (both scientific and fictional).

Selected Bibliography

Davis, Randall W., and Anthony M. Pagano, eds.
*Ethology and Behavioral Ecology of Sea Otters and
Polar Bears.* New York: Springer, 2021.

Kruuk, Hans. *Otters: Ecology, Behaviour and Conservation.*
Oxford, UK: Oxford University Press, 2006.

McLeish, Todd. *Return of the Sea Otter: The Story of the
Animal that Evaded Extinction on the Pacific Coast.*
Seattle, WA: Sasquatch Books, 2018.

Palumbi, Stephen R., and Carolyn Sotka. *The Death and
Life of Monterey Bay: A Story of Revival.* Washington,
DC: Island Press, 2011.

Ravalli, Richard. *Sea Otters: A History.* Lincoln:
University of Nebraska Press, 2018.

Thomas, Tim, and Dennis Copeland. *Images of
America: Monterey's Waterfront.* Charleston, SC:
Arcadia Publishing, 2006.

resources for young readers

print

Buhrman-Deever, Susannah. *If You Take Away the Otter.* Somerville, MA: Candlewick Press, 2020.

Groc, Isabelle. *Sea Otters: A Survival Story.* Victoria, BC: Orca Book Publishers, 2020.

Hall, Howard. *Jean-Michel Cousteau Presents: The Secrets of Kelp Forests: Life's Ebb and Flow in the Sea's Richest Habitat.* Montrose, CA: London Town Press, 2007.

Newman, Patricia. *Sea Otter Heroes: The Predators that Saved an Ecosystem.* Minneapolis, MN: Millbrook Press, 2017.

Riedman, Marianne. *Sea Otters.* Monterey, CA: Monterey Bay Aquarium, 1990.

Rothman, Julia. *Ocean Anatomy: The Curious Parts and Pieces of the World Under the Sea.* North Adams, MA: Storey Publishing, 2020.

online

Monterey Bay Aquarium: montereybayaquarium.org

Monterey Bay Aquarium Sea Otter Cam:
montereybayaquarium.org/animals/live-cams
/sea-otter-cam

Elkhorn Slough OtterCam: elkhornslough.org/
ottercam

Thank you for reading this Feiwel & Friends book.
The friends who made *Odder* possible are:

Jean Feiwel, Publisher
Liz Szabla, VP, Associate Publisher
Rich Deas, Senior Creative Director
Holly West, Senior Editor
Anna Roberto, Senior Editor
Kat Brzozowski, Senior Editor
Dawn Ryan, Executive Managing Editor
Kim Waymer, Senior Production Manager
Emily Settle, Editor
Rachel Diebel, Associate Editor
Foyinsi Adegbonmire, Associate Editor
Brittany Groves, Assistant Editor
Mallory Grigg, Senior Art Director
Helen Seachrist, Senior Production Editor

Follow us on Facebook or visit us online at
mackids.com. Our books are friends for life.

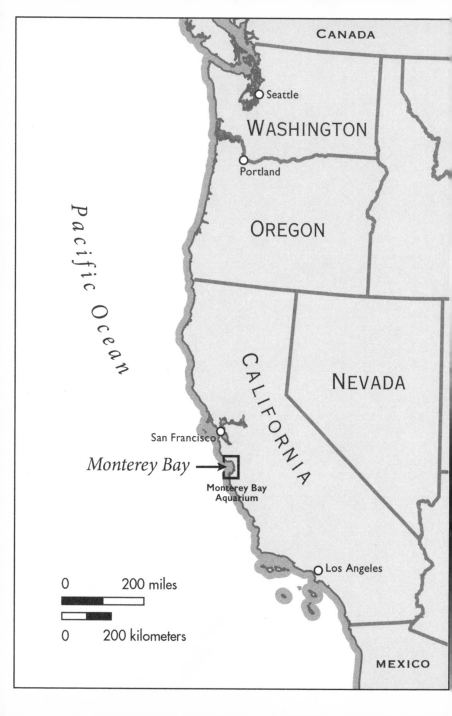